PRIME Baby

PRIME Baby

Gene Luen Yang

Colors by
Derek Kirk Kim

Here's me at my 6th birthday party two years ago, back when the world still made sense.

Ha, ha. Look at this one. Happy as a pig in slop. I told my parents not to invite anyone from school so I could have the whole cake to myself.

The old lady behind me is my grandma. I let her come because she's diabetic.

What a poor fool I was, blissful in my own ignorance. Little did I know how different things would be a mere six months later—

—when *she* came along.

My mother's womb is a Trojan horse, I tell you.

My folks call her an "unexpected blessing." Please. If it walks like an accident and talks like an accident, let's just call it an accident, all right?

Smile, Maddie!

I know what you're thinking. You think I'm just jealous of all the attention those fat little baby cheeks of hers are getting. But that's not it. That's not it at all.

snap!
FLASH!

Ha, ha! So cute!

My disdain for her is much more rational.

See, she's going on 18 months now. At this point, most babies are babbling all sorts of nonsense. An elite few—like me when I was her age—have even started speaking words. Our precious little Maddie?

ga

That's it. Seriously. No "ooh." No "ah." No "mama" or "papa." Just "ga," over and over and over again.

All day.
Ga ga.
All night.
Ga ga ga ga ga ga ga ga ga ga ga ga ga ga ga.
Is that a sign of something mental or what?
When I mention this to my mom, she replies with typical adult spin.
Each person develops at her own pace, Thaddeus, and that's perfectly O.K.
Mom, you and Dad gotta face facts. That baby's ***dumb in the head.***
Thaddeus K. Fong: Martyr for Truth.

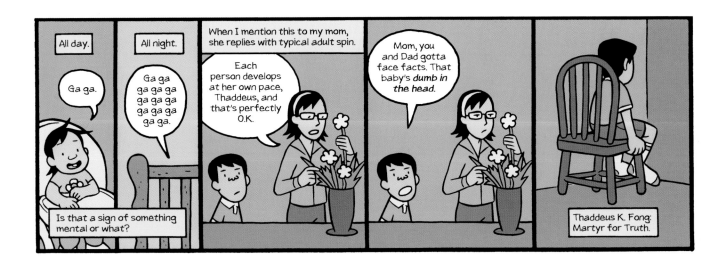

These days, Fu Manchu is considered an icon of early-20th-century racism, but personally I admire the guy.
As you all should know from your homework last night, a prime number can be divided only by one and itself.
I mean, who doesn't want to take over the world? Our man Fu just had the guts to do something about it.
Heck, they even named a mustache after him.
What are you drawing?
That's Rosie Yi. I find her incredibly annoying, but I put up with it.
When we get to high school, Rosie will most likely be built like a brick house. I've seen her mom.
It's a facial-hair configuration I'm calling "the Thaddeus."

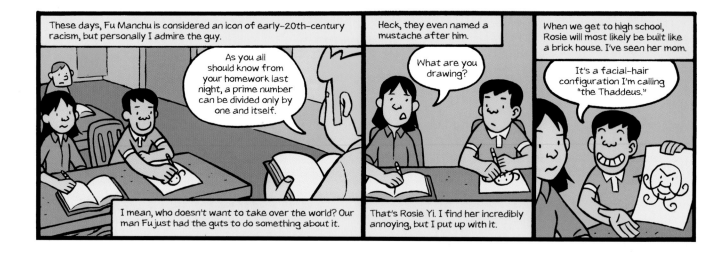

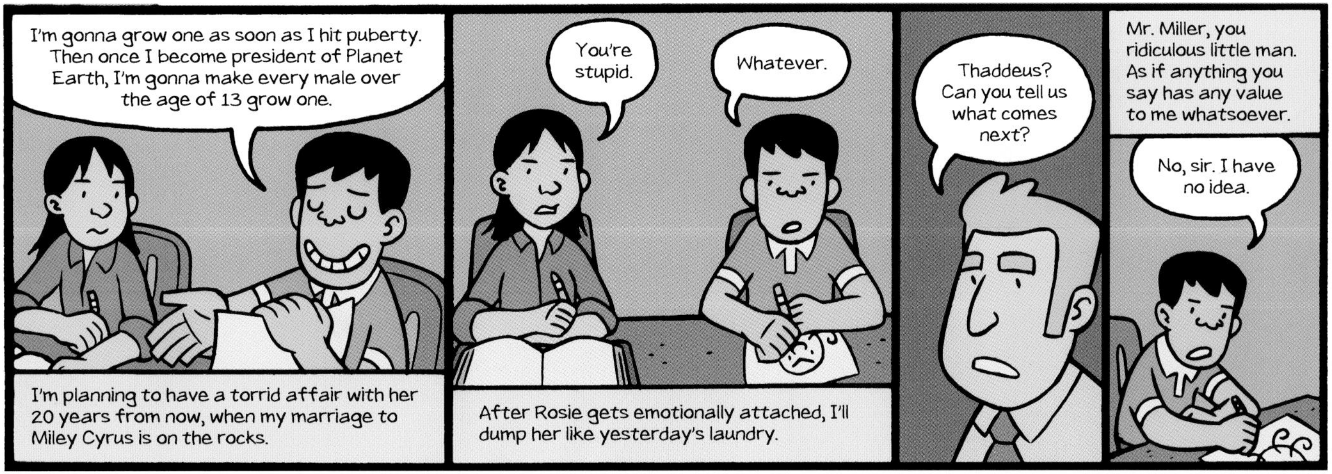
I'm gonna grow one as soon as I hit puberty. Then once I become president of Planet Earth, I'm gonna make every male over the age of 13 grow one.
I'm planning to have a torrid affair with her 20 years from now, when my marriage to Miley Cyrus is on the rocks.
You're stupid.
Whatever.
After Rosie gets emotionally attached, I'll dump her like yesterday's laundry.
Thaddeus? Can you tell us what comes next?
Mr. Miller, you ridiculous little man. As if anything you say has any value to me whatsoever.
No, sir. I have no idea.

Seven, Thaddeus. Next is seven. Then 11, then 13. And there you have the first six prime numbers.
How's this ever gonna be useful in real life?
Ha, ha. Good one, Rosie. Maybe we can have a love child together before I break your heart.
I'm glad you asked, Ms. Yi. Prime numbers rarely occur in nature, but any society with reasonably developed mathematics can deduce what they are.
2 3 5 7
11 13
In fact, NASA scientists have theorized that if aliens were ever to make contact with us, it would be through prime numbers.
!
Mr. Miller! I stand corrected! You **have** taught me something of value!
You've taught me the truth about my baby sister.
1 Ga 2 ga 3 ga 4 ga 5 ga 6 ga 7 ga.

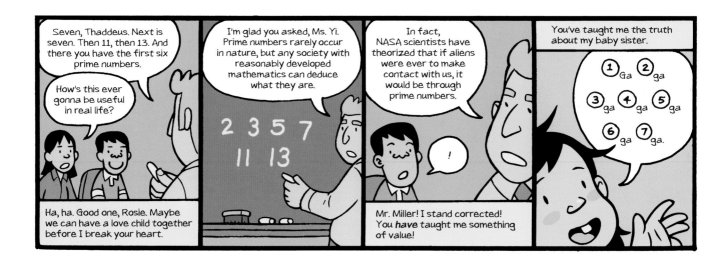

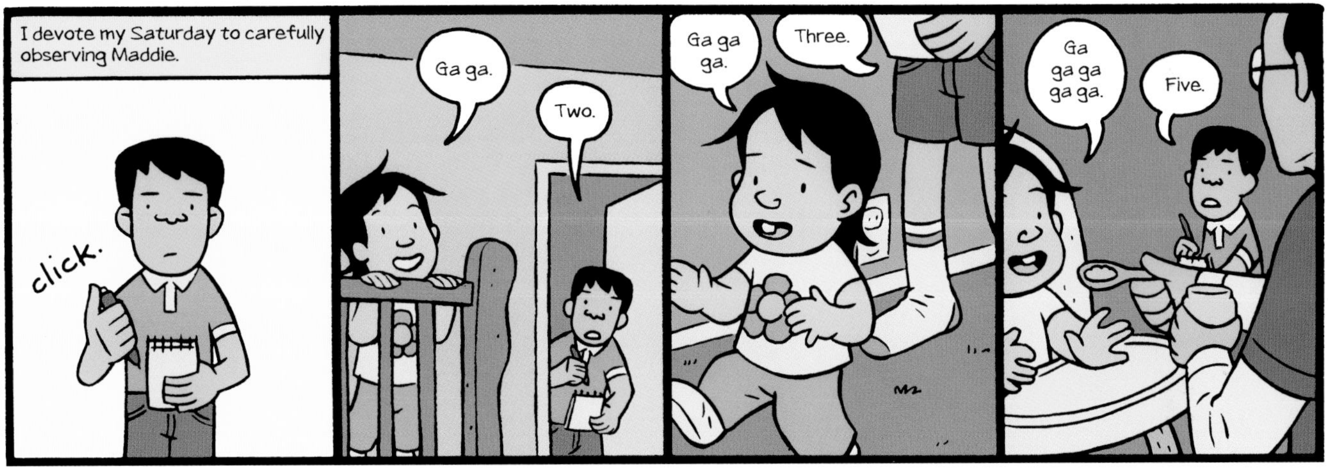
I devote my Saturday to carefully observing Maddie.
click.
Ga ga.
Two.
Ga ga ga.
Three.
Ga ga ga ga ga.
Five.

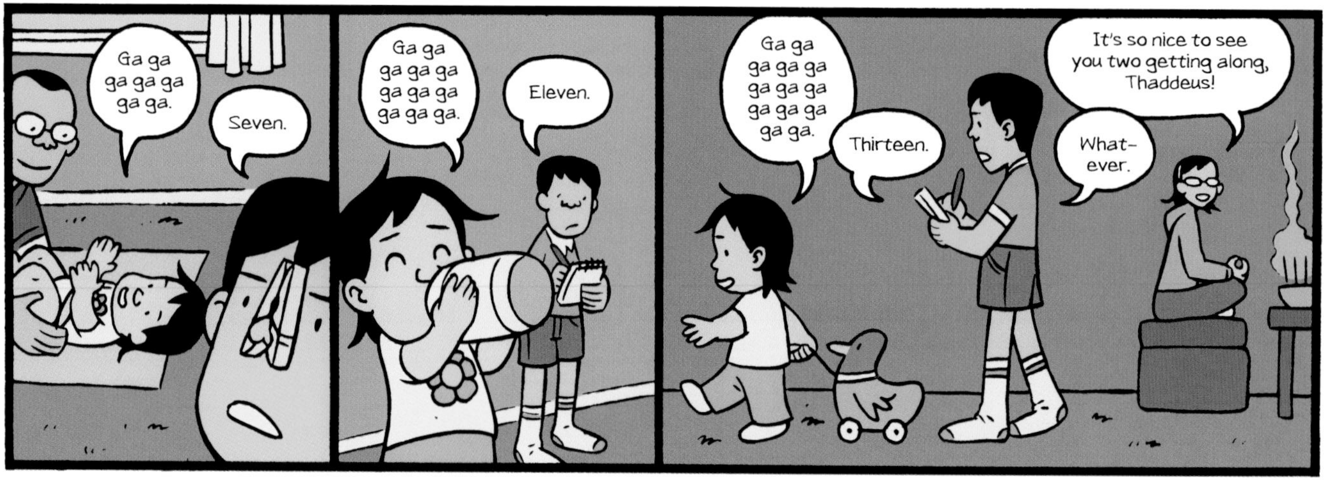
Ga ga ga ga ga ga ga.
Seven.
Ga ga ga ga ga ga ga ga ga ga ga.
Eleven.
Ga ga ga ga ga ga ga ga ga ga ga ga ga ga.
Thirteen.
It's so nice to see you two getting along, Thaddeus!
What-ever.

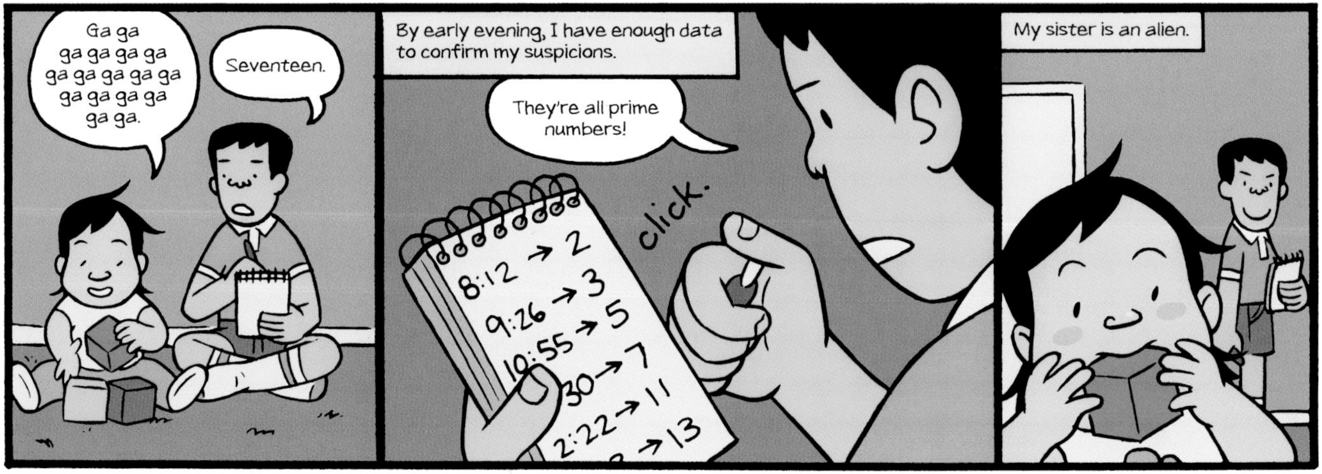
Ga ga
ga ga ga ga
ga ga ga ga ga
ga ga ga ga
ga ga.
Seventeen.
By early evening, I have enough data to confirm my suspicions.
They're all prime numbers!
8:12 → 2
9:26 → 3
10:55 → 5
2:22 → 11
→ 13
click.
My sister is an alien.

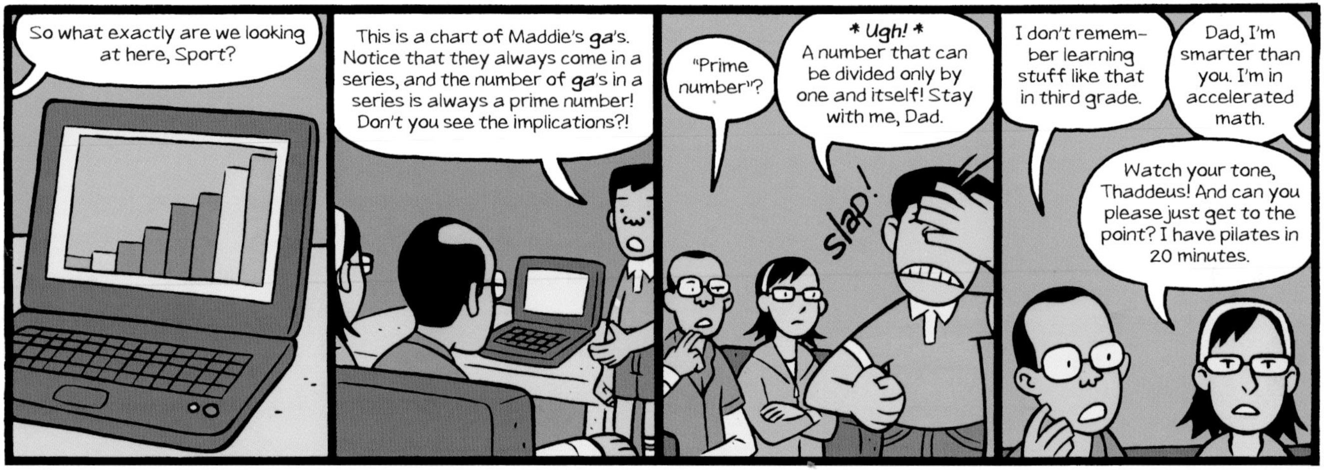
So what exactly are we looking at here, Sport?
This is a chart of Maddie's **ga**'s. Notice that they always come in a series, and the number of **ga**'s in a series is always a prime number! Don't you see the implications?!
"Prime number"?
* Ugh! * A number that can be divided only by one and itself! Stay with me, Dad.
slap!
I don't remem-ber learning stuff like that in third grade.
Dad, I'm smarter than you. I'm in accelerated math.
Watch your tone, Thaddeus! And can you please just get to the point? I have pilates in 20 minutes.

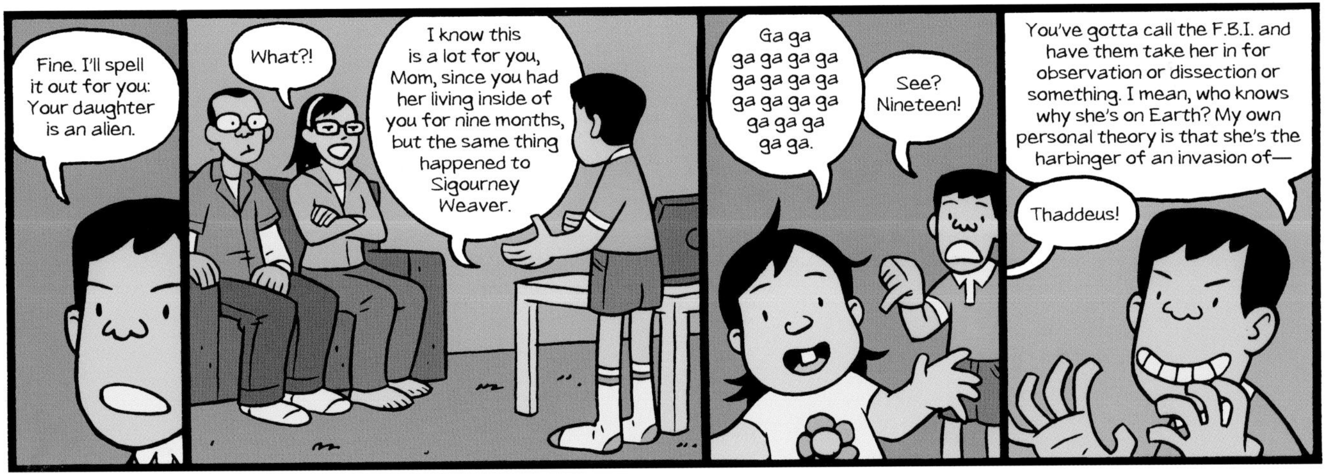
Fine. I'll spell it out for you: Your daughter is an alien.
What?!
I know this is a lot for you, Mom, since you had her living inside of you for nine months, but the same thing happened to Sigourney Weaver.
Ga ga ga ga ga ga ga ga ga ga ga ga ga ga ga ga ga ga ga.
See? Nineteen!
You've gotta call the F.B.I. and have them take her in for observation or dissection or something. I mean, who knows why she's on Earth? My own personal theory is that she's the harbinger of an invasion of—
Thaddeus!

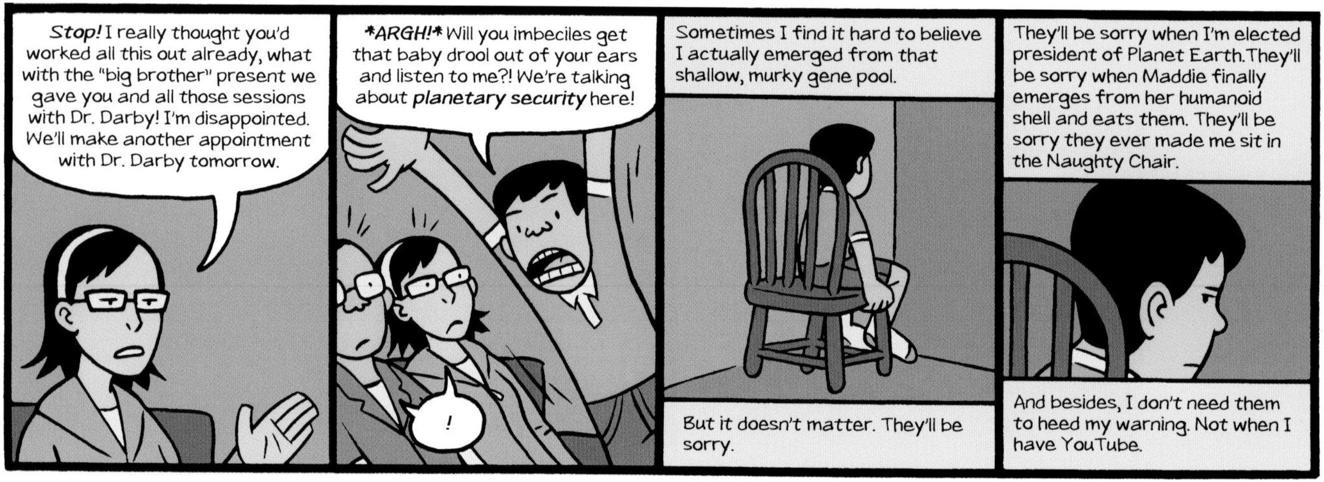
Stop! I really thought you'd worked all this out already, what with the "big brother" present we gave you and all those sessions with Dr. Darby! I'm disappointed. We'll make another appointment with Dr. Darby tomorrow.
ARGH! Will you imbeciles get that baby drool out of your ears and listen to me?! We're talking about planetary security here!
!
Sometimes I find it hard to believe I actually emerged from that shallow, murky gene pool.
But it doesn't matter. They'll be sorry.
They'll be sorry when I'm elected president of Planet Earth. They'll be sorry when Maddie finally emerges from her humanoid shell and eats them. They'll be sorry they ever made me sit in the Naughty Chair.
And besides, I don't need them to heed my warning. Not when I have YouTube.

Panel 1: My parents bought this camcorder a couple of months before Maddie was born, intent on capturing every gas-induced smile she managed to eke out. They forbade me from ever touching it.

All right, Maddie. Do your thing.

Panel 2: As if what happened to the plasma screen was entirely my fault.

Ga ga ga.

Good. Keep going.

Panel 3: So I'm kind of disobeying my parents. So what? Excuse me for choosing the very survival of our species over their silly, small-minded rules.

Come on.

Panel 4: History will vindicate me.

Maddie! Pay attention! You know what comes next!

"Ga ga ga ga ga!"

!

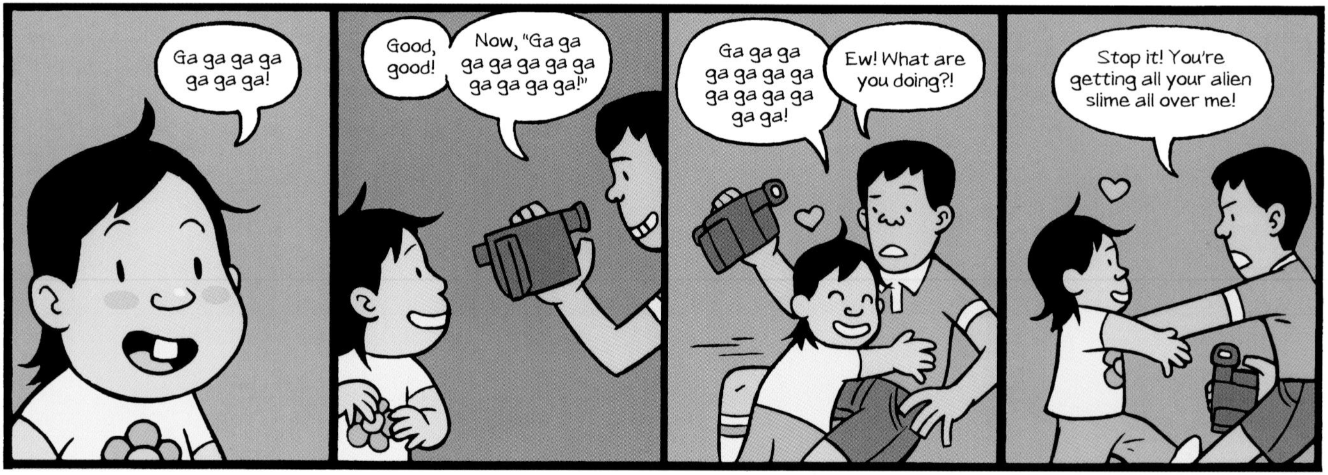
Ga ga ga ga ga ga ga!
Good, good!
Now, "Ga ga ga ga ga ga ga ga ga ga ga!"
Ga ga ga ga ga ga ga ga ga ga ga ga ga!
Ew! What are you doing?!
Stop it! You're getting all your alien slime all over me!

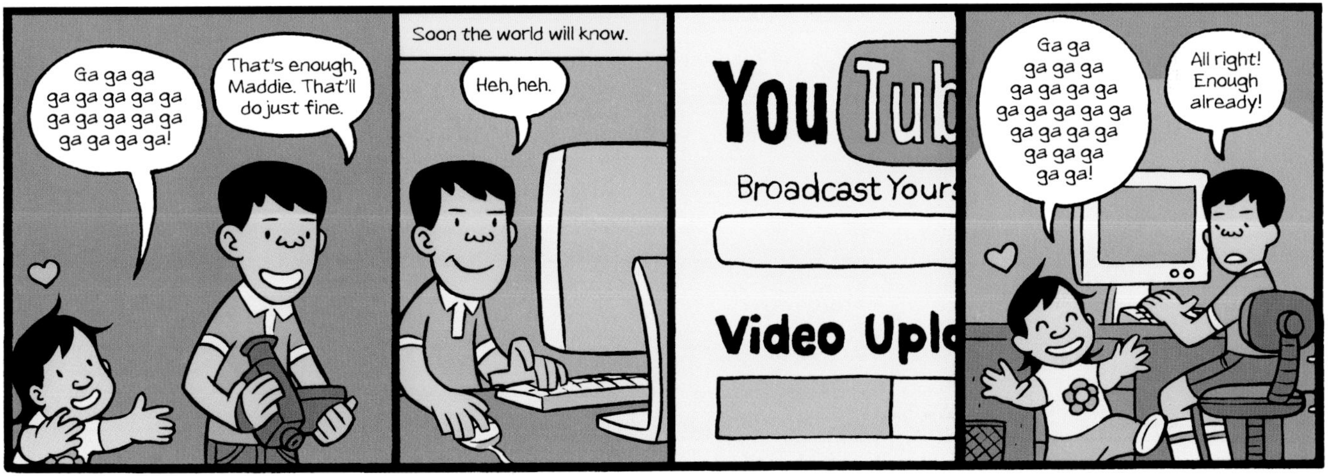
Ga ga ga ga ga ga ga ga ga ga ga ga ga ga ga ga ga ga!
That's enough, Maddie. That'll do just fine.
Soon the world will know.
Heh, heh.
YouTub
Broadcast Yours
Video Uplo
Ga ga ga ga ga ga ga ga ga ga ga ga ga ga ga ga ga ga ga ga ga ga ga ga ga ga!
All right! Enough already!

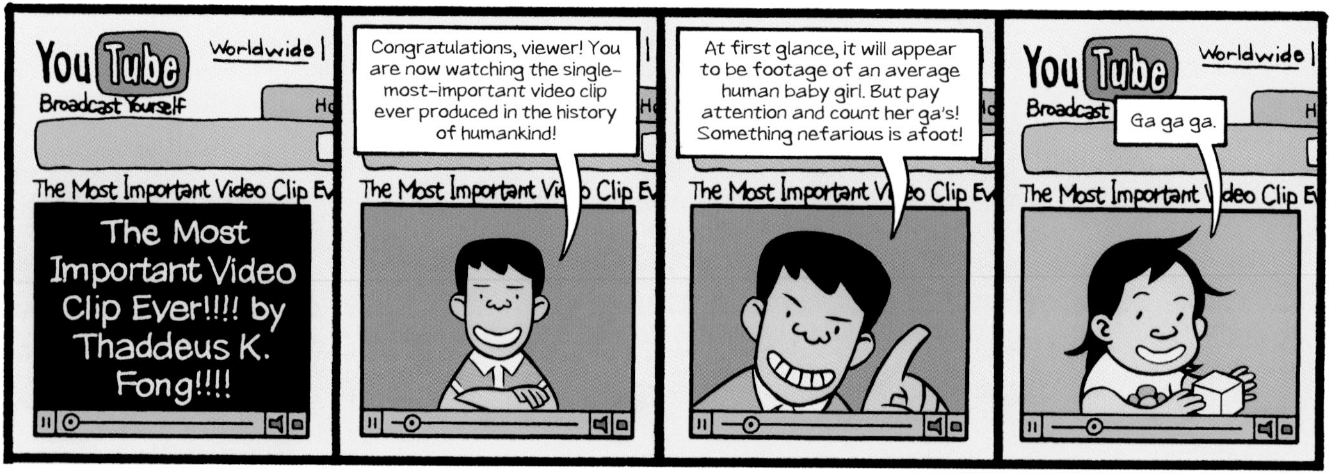
YouTube
Broadcast Yourself
Worldwide
The Most Important Video Clip Ev
The Most Important Video Clip Ever!!!! by Thaddeus K. Fong!!!!
Congratulations, viewer! You are now watching the single-most-important video clip ever produced in the history of humankind!
At first glance, it will appear to be footage of an average human baby girl. But pay attention and count her ga's! Something nefarious is afoot!
Ga ga ga.

Worldwide
Ga ga ga ga ga ga ga!
The Most Important Video Clip Ev
Worldwide
Ga ga ga ga ga ga ga ga ga ga ga ga ga!
See? First 3, then 7, then 13! All prime numbers! How could a human baby possibly understand a complex mathematical concept like prime numbers, you ask?
The answer is ... your very question is flawed! She is ***not*** a human baby! She is in fact an alien, the harbinger of an extraterrestrial invasion of epic proportions!

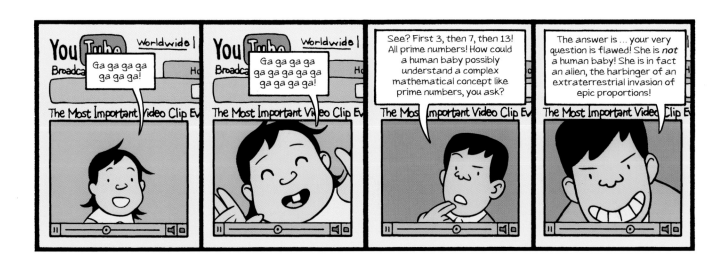

YouTube
Broadcast Yourself
Worldwide |
The Most Important Video Clip Ev
The Most Important Video Clip Ever!!!! by Thaddeus K. Fong!!!!
Important Video Clip Ever!!!! by Thaddeus K. Fong!!!!
Rate:
▽ Text Comments (4)
Shiga11 (11 minutes ago)
freakazoid !!!!!!
Rate:
▽ Text Comments (4)
Shiga11 (11 minutes ago)
freakazoid !!!!!!
rock_biter (30 minutes ag
dude dat fools n my class
hrududu98 (3 hours ag
OMG! cute baby!

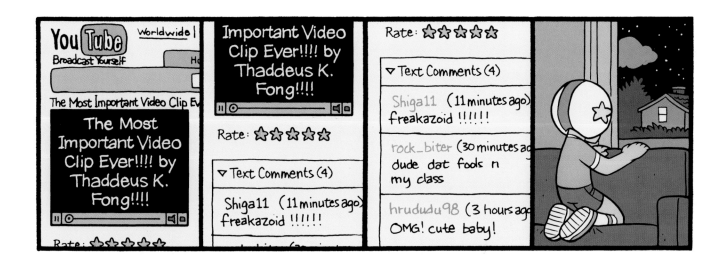

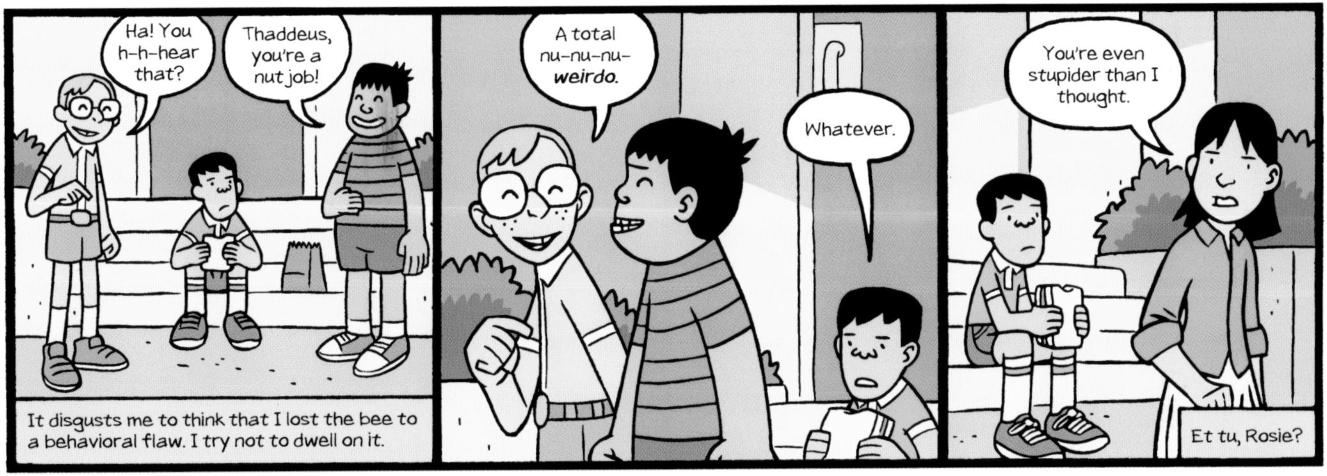
Ha! You h-h-hear that?
Thaddeus, you're a nut job!
It disgusts me to think that I lost the bee to a behavioral flaw. I try not to dwell on it.
A total nu-nu-nu- **weirdo**.
Whatever.
You're even stupider than I thought.
Et tu, Rosie?

22

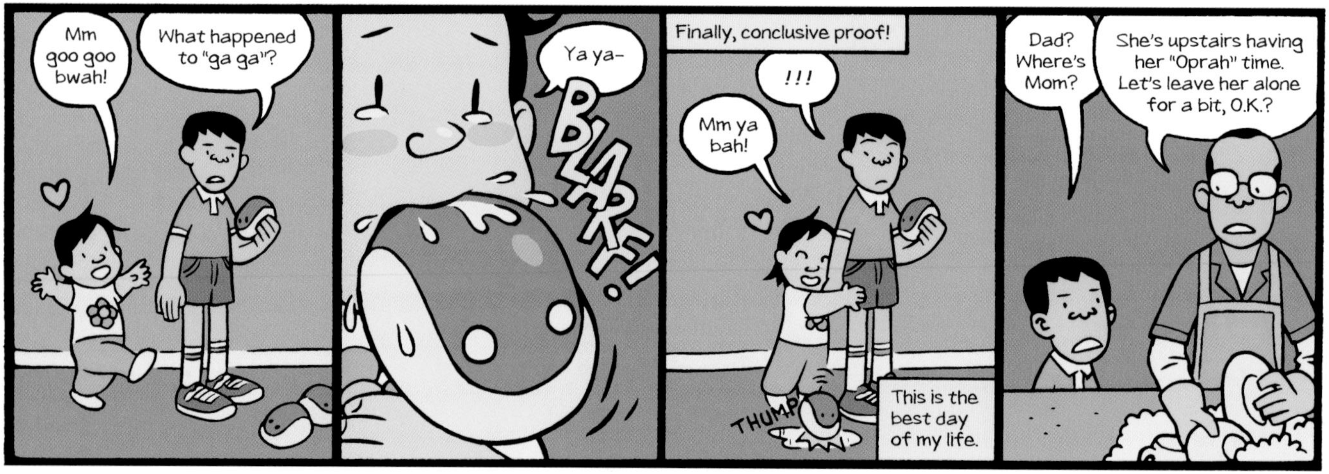
Mm goo goo bwah!
What happened to "ga ga"?
Ya ya-
BLARF!
Finally, conclusive proof!
!!!
Mm ya bah!
THUMP
This is the best day of my life.
Dad? Where's Mom?
She's upstairs having her "Oprah" time. Let's leave her alone for a bit, O.K.?

25

26

My parents—and all the world—will adore me forever.
What a guy!
He's the best thing I ever gave birth to!
My presidency of Planet Earth will be all but assured.
Miley, ***please!*** Not in front of the cameras!
Bap mmm?
Ya ya bap mmm ya!
After all those space pods came out of her, Maddie has inexplicably become a normal baby.
Which is totally fine by me. She's no longer part of the equation.
Maddie, leave me alone!

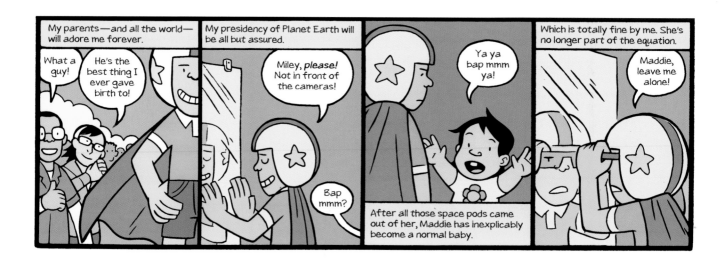

It's just past midnight when I finally finish both my costume and arsenal.

I've decided this is the perfect opportunity to introduce the world to "the Thaddeus," that mustache I invented.

I needed a little help from my mom's eyeliner. Notoriety does not wait for puberty, unfortunately.

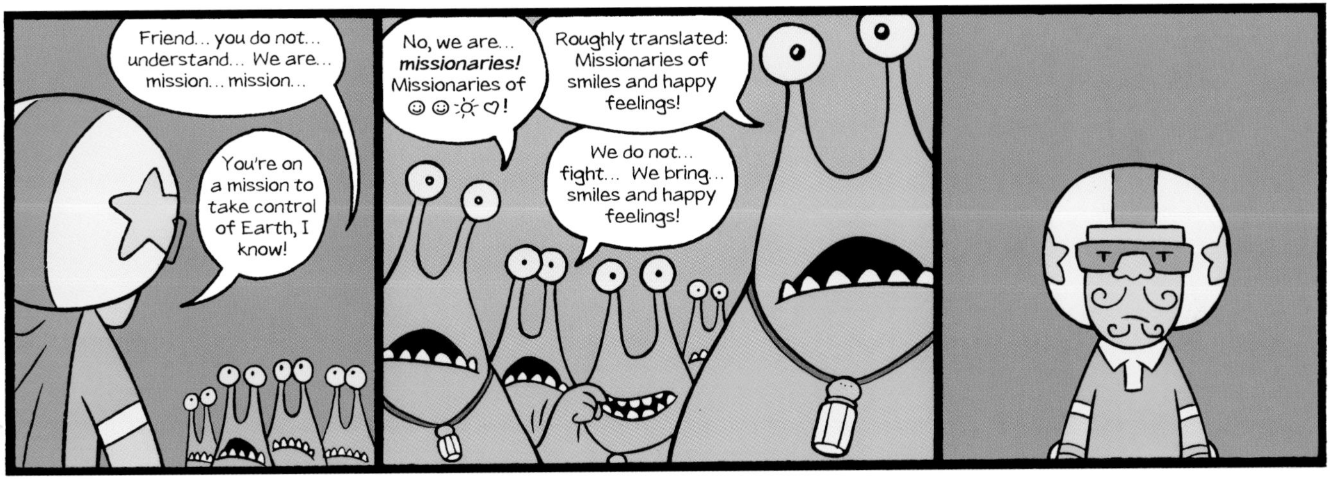
Friend... you do not... understand... We are... mission... mission...
You're on a mission to take control of Earth, I know!
No, we are... *missionaries!* Missionaries of ☺ ☺ ☼ ♡!
Roughly translated: Missionaries of smiles and happy feelings!
We do not... fight... We bring... smiles and happy feelings!

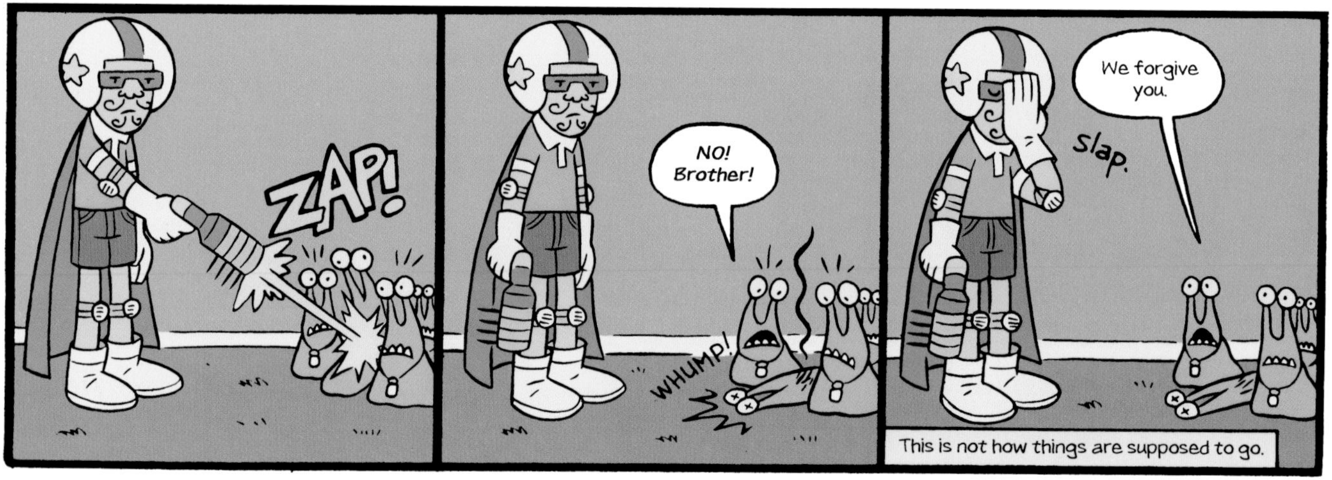
ZAP!
NO! Brother!
WHUMP!
We forgive you.
Slap.
This is not how things are supposed to go.

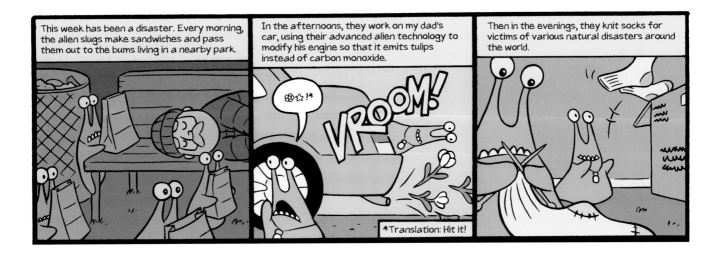

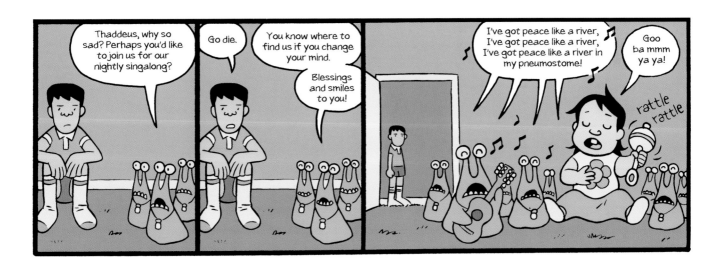

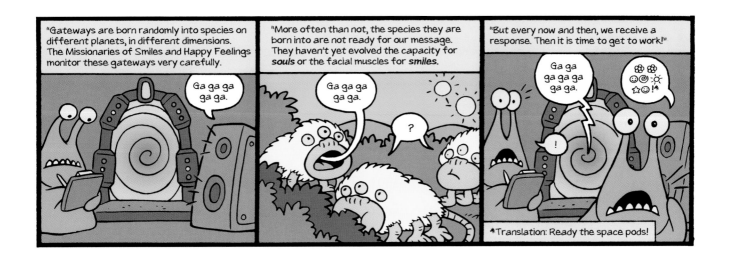

37

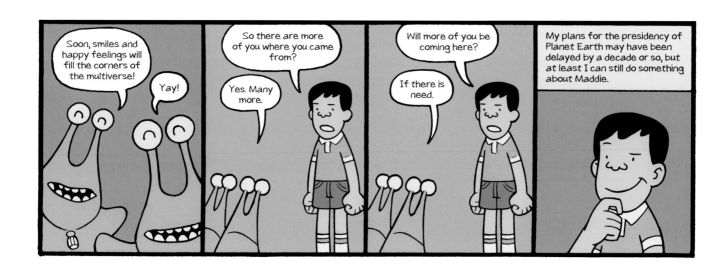

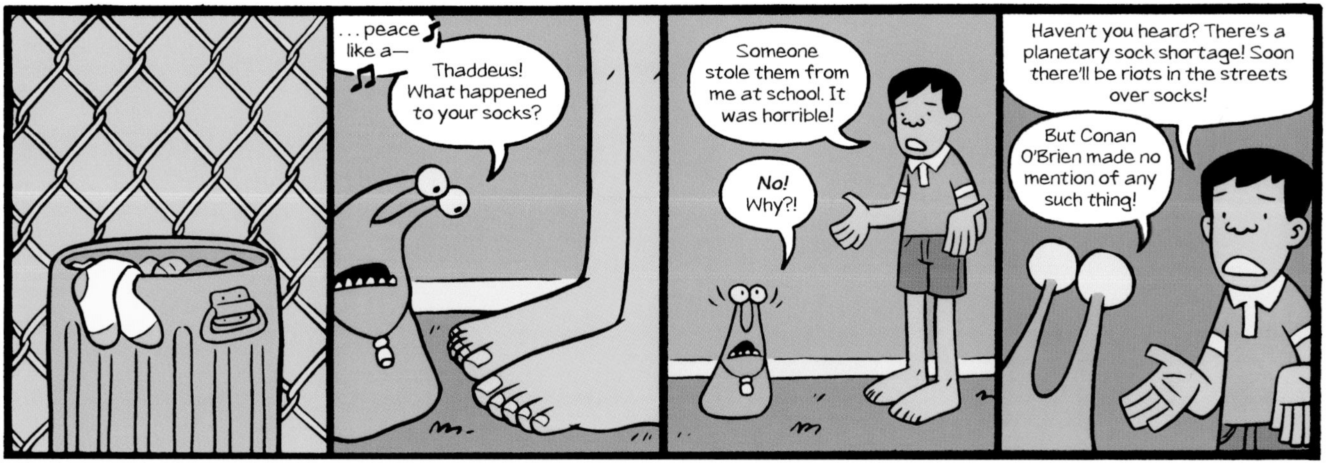
. . . peace like a—
Thaddeus! What happened to your socks?
Someone stole them from me at school. It was horrible!
No! Why?!
Haven't you heard? There's a planetary sock shortage! Soon there'll be riots in the streets over socks!
But Conan O'Brien made no mention of any such thing!

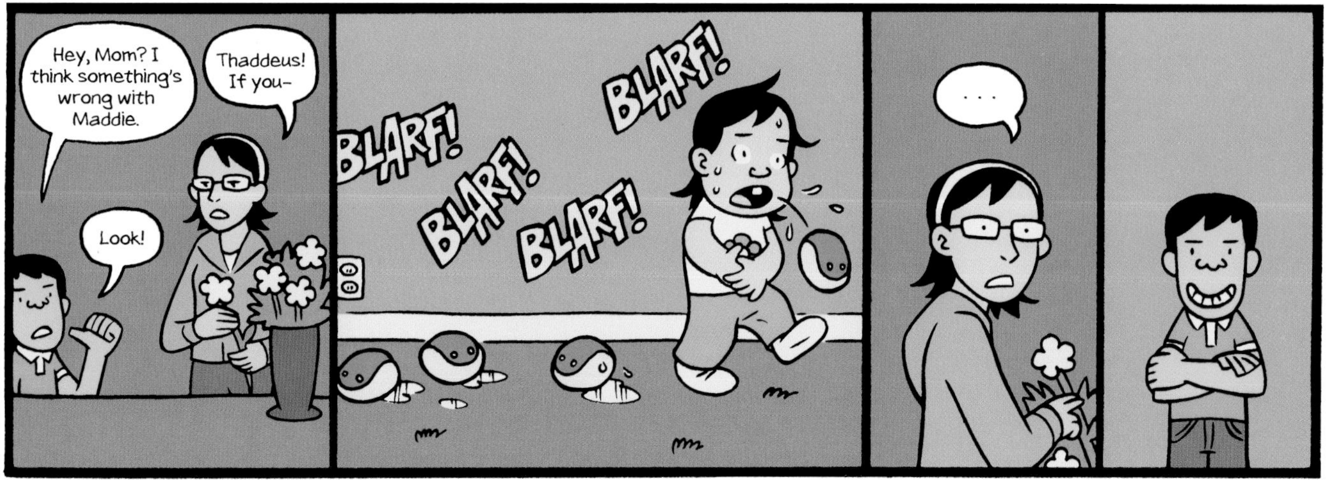
Hey, Mom? I think something's wrong with Maddie.
Thaddeus! If you–
Look!
BLARF!
BLARF!
BLARF!
BLARF!
. . .

My parents took Maddie to the emergency room last week. During the examination, the doctor accidentally dropped her tongue depressor into the alien slug dimension. Government agents were called in.

Maddie's now being kept in a secret underground research facility, accessible only through a fake wall in the broom closet of a Vietnamese nail salon downtown.

The space pods have been sent three floors below, where a group of eggheads are undoubtedly wetting their pants over them.

Excuse me, ma'am.

Again, Jones?

So sorry, ma'am. It's just too exciting.

My parents insist on visiting her every day. Even with the 12-inch-thick Plexiglas wall separating us from Maddie, they make us wear Hazmat suits.

Hazmat suits! *So awesome.*

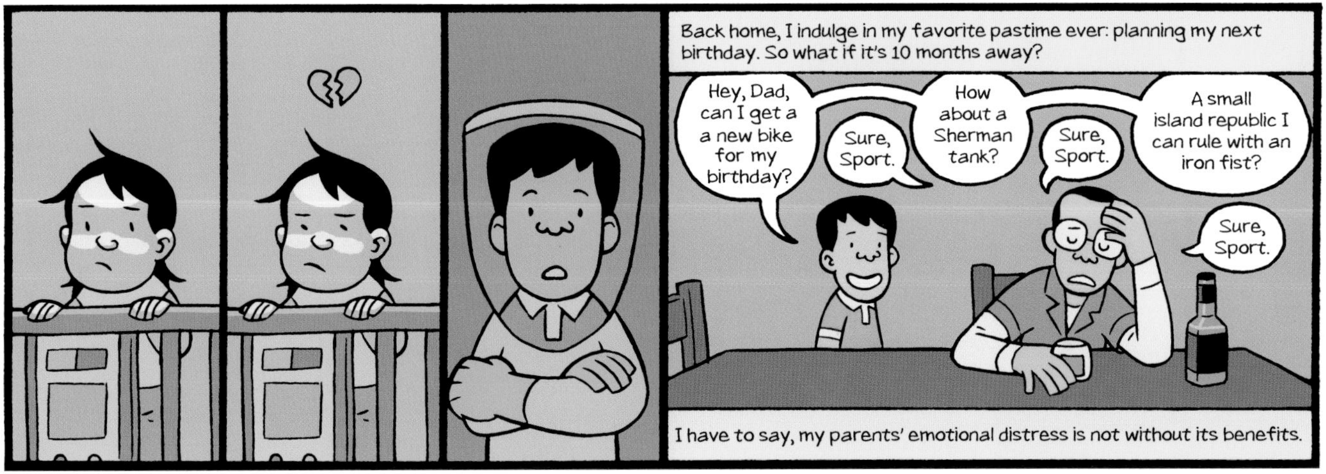

Back home, I indulge in my favorite pastime ever: planning my next birthday. So what if it's 10 months away?
Hey, Dad, can I get a a new bike for my birthday?
Sure, Sport.
How about a Sherman tank?
Sure, Sport.
A small island republic I can rule with an iron fist?
Sure, Sport.
I have to say, my parents' emotional distress is not without its benefits.

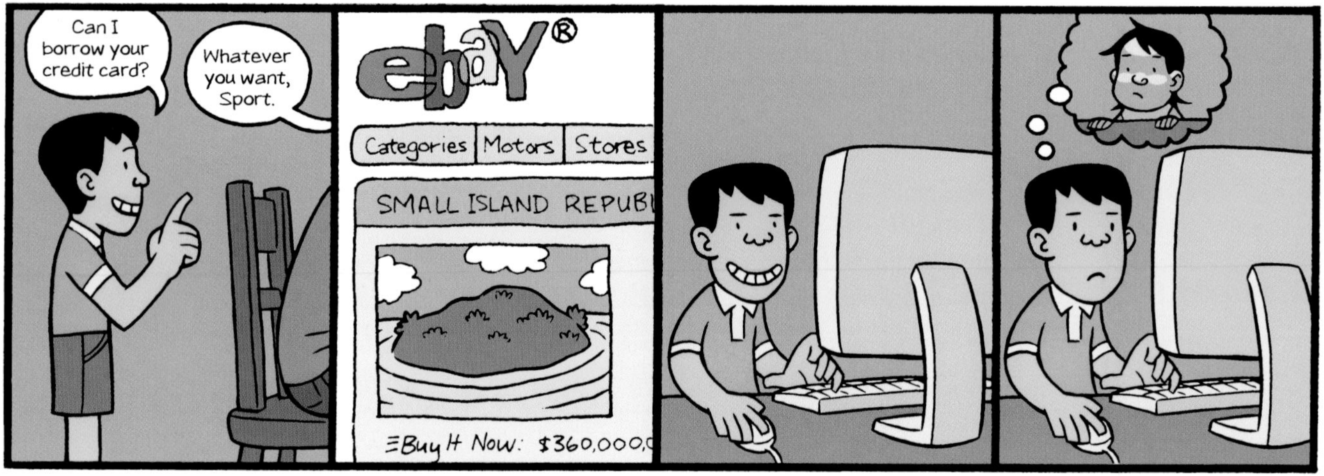
Can I borrow your credit card?
Whatever you want, Sport.
ebaY®
Categories
Motors
Stores
SMALL ISLAND REPUBL
Buy It Now: $360,000,0

OOF!
Ha, ha! Tell me, Stan, how many P's are there in "whupped"?
WHAM!
Suddenly, without really meaning to or wanting to, I recognize that look Maddie gave me during our last visit to the research facility.
Loneliness.
WHAM!

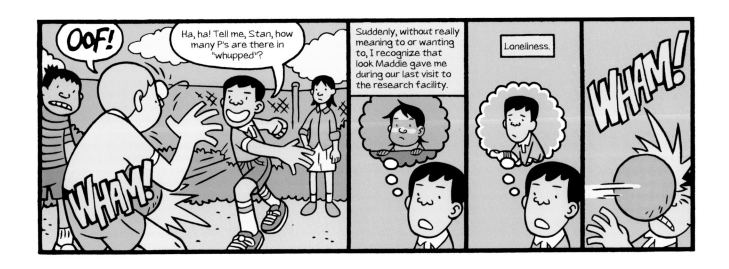

What the-?!
You lied to us!
We called in countless missionaries to spend countless hours knitting countless socks, all to relieve a worldwide sock shortage that doesn't even exist! We are so *angry!*
But we forgive you.
Yeah.

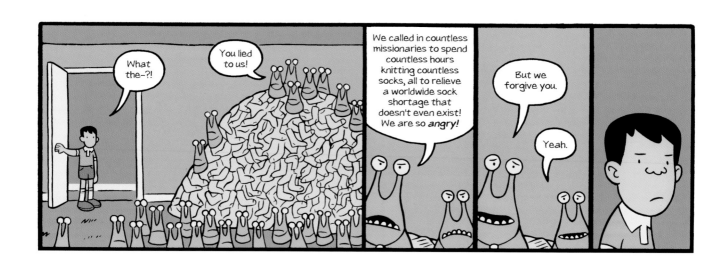

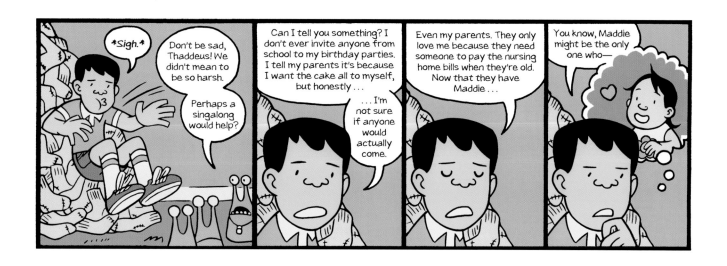

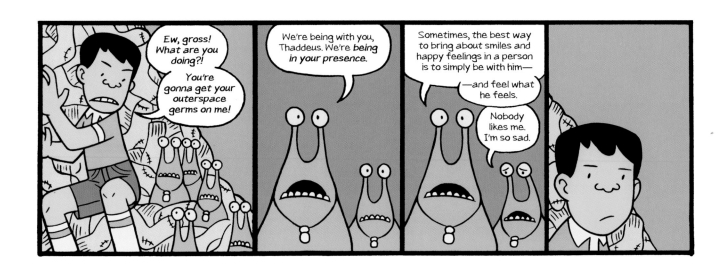

After Maddie was taken to the secret underground research facility, my parents swept through our house gathering up all the space pods they could find.

They handed them over to the government, hoping it might get Maddie released sooner.

Yeah. As if the government ever does anything "sooner."

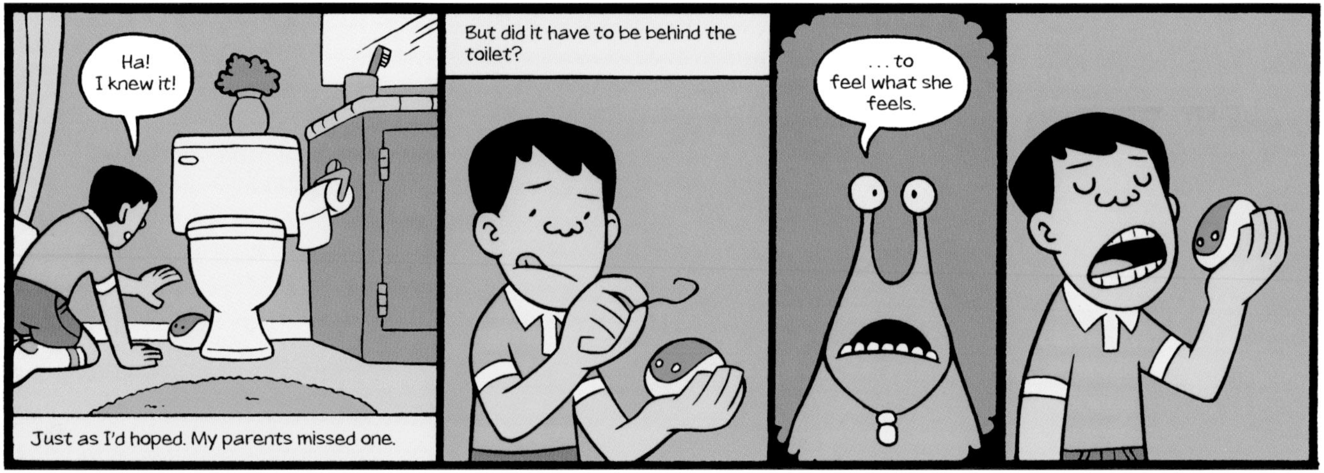
Ha! I knew it!
Just as I'd hoped. My parents missed one.
But did it have to be behind the toilet?
. . . to feel what she feels.

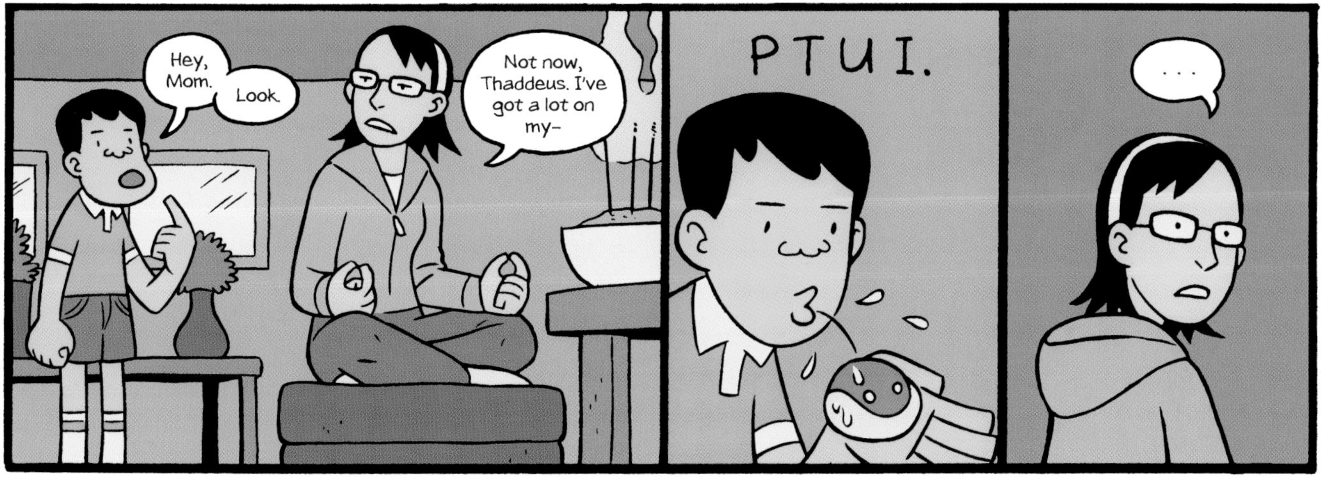
Hey, Mom.
Look.
Not now, Thaddeus. I've got a lot on my-
PTUI.
...

56

First Second

New York & London

First published in the *New York Times Magazine*. Copyright © 2008, 2009 by Gene Luen Yang. Compilation Copyright © 2010 by Gene Luen Yang.

Published by First Second,
First Second is an imprint of Roaring Brook Press, a division of Holtzbrinck Publishing Holdings Limited Partnership,
175 Fifth Avenue, New York, NY 10010

Distributed in Canada by H. B. Fenn and Company Ltd.
distributed in the United Kingdom by Macmillan Children's Books, a division of Pan Macmillan.

Colored by Derek Kirk Kim
Design by Colleen AF Venable

Cataloging-in-Publication Data is on file at the Library of Congress.
ISBN: 978-1-59643-612-1
COLLECTOR'S EDITION ISBN: 978-1-59643-650-3

First Second books are available for special promotions and premiums. For details, contact: Director of Special Markets, Holtzbrinck Publishers.

First Edition April 2010
Printed in China
10 9 8 7 6 5 4 3 2 1